Spark

That Ignites You

Publication House

"Spark that Ignites You"

ISBN No: " 978-93-90416-75-2"
1st Edition
Language – English and Hindi

Flairs and Glairs
Publication House
Regd. Under MSME Act.

Disclaimer

This is a work of fiction and solely represent the thoughts of the corresponding authors of the articles. Our editors have tried their best to edit the content of all the authors and check the plagiarism.

All the write-ups in this book are unique and are only published in this book.

In case any plagiarism or error is found, only the author is responsible alone, and not the publisher or the Compilers.

Cover Designing and Book Formatting
Shubham Shah

Acknowledgement

Dear Almighty, thank you for blessing me with the power and zeal to be able to complete this Anthology. Also, Thank You dear parents, for trusting in me, and letting me work whenever I wanted. My family is the one who supported me for what I am today.
When it comes to this Anthology, I would like to start with Thanking the Co-authors, without your help and support, I would have never been able to complete it.

Thank You all of you, for being there. Much Love to all of You. I am glad to see you all standing by me.

Co Author

1. Shubham Shah (Founder and Compiler)
2. Ishani Agarwal (Co Founder)
3. Ishika Agarwal
4. Ashima Jain
5. Gousia Ajaz Khan
6. Kartikeya Chauhan
7. Reettika Premjit
8. Vidhya Lakshmi
9. Nardhana Ramakrishnan
10. Natasha Sahoo
11. Vijay Appaji
12. Vidisha Agrawal
13. Leena Saththi
14. Sahina Mamtaz Chowdhury
15. Nishigandha Das
16. Akhil Kumar Singh
17. Shri Sambhabi Mishra
18. Archa
19. Harsha Sharma
20. Pragya Rani
21. Abdur Razzaque
22. Sneha Kumari
23. Riya Ghosh
24. Singhetampravalika (S.Pravalika)
25. Deenu S Adi

26. Shakti Sinha
27. Cuan Damons
28. Parul Saxena 'Kehkasha'
29. Punit Dubey
30. Kancharla Sai Sandeep
31. Priyadharshini(Abi)
32. Deborah Esther
33. Ayushi
34. Ayush Manot
35. Deepanshi Sarwal
36. Bheemparam Kishore Kumar
37. Soumith Reddy Pingili
38. Mahammad Rizwan Ahamed

Shubham Shah

(Founder- Flairs and Glairs)
(Compiler)

Shubham Shah, entrepreneur at "Flairs & Glairs" a brand with dynamics in events organizing and cultural educational pan INDIA, He is a 26yr. old guy who recently has entered, the digital platform of imprinting emotions. He has initiated with his own open mic platform to help budding poets and aspiring writers under his brand named as "Teekhe Zasbaaat"
He is a commerce graduate from Bhagalpur City of Bihar.
He says Writing has impersonated him since childhood and he has now been writing for over a decade!

Cooking, on the other hand, is his passion! He also mentions, trying out new things just tickles him!
When asked sir, Why SPICY EMOTIONS?
He smiled and added, “agar jasbaat teekhe na ho toh wo jasbaat kaha” Spices are all that blends! So do his words!
As a chef, he presents to you his dish! Hot and freshly served! Taste it! Feel it! Enjoy it! You can also find his writing in the Solo book “Teekhe Zasbaaat” and 70+ anthologies. With his passion to explore opportunities across Platforms he is working with keen devotion and We wish him all the very best for his future ventures
Share your reviews on his

INSTAGRAM

@spicy_emotions
@shubham4shah

Or via email on

shubham2shah@gmail.com

To stay tuned to his work and opportunities follow his business Handles

INSTAGRAM FACEBOOK YOUTUBE

@flairsandglairs
@teekhezasbaaat

WEBSITE:

https://flairsandglairs.in/
https://flairsandglairs.com/

Kar khwaishein asi ki parwardigar bhi puche aarzoo teri...
Dikha himmat ki puche khuda raza teri...
Ankho me ankhe dal kar puche sake nakamiyabiyo par...
ki kya galati rahi teri...

Rakh himmat badha kadam...
Kar hausla buland...
Nak mastak rehkar rakh apna khun garam...

Ubal rakh...

Narmi teri garmi ko palna sikhaegi...
Gusse ko teri urja banaegi...
Bulandiyon tak tujhe pahuchaegi...

Bikhra hai na aj tu...
Tujhe muqamaal banaegi...
Galiyon ke shor ko taaliyon ki goonj banaegi...

Ishani Agarwal

(Co Founder- Flairs and Glairs)

Ishani Agarwal
Born and brought up in Kolkata, she has done her schooling and college from here itself. She is doing her post-graduation at the moment. Ishani loves talking to people around, and is excited for this new beginning of hers! Been a Compiler for 35+ Anthologies, and in the process for more, also, co-authored in 100+ Anthologies, Ishani is very Happy with how her life is turning out now!
Insta handle: Ishani_agarwal_quotes

Mood Spoils..

This person never understood her..
He would never understand what she was trying to say..
Always wanted her to be direct..
Thinking of this, she recalled the last fight she had with her boyfriend..
With a sour mood she called him that night,
And his lack of understanding spoiled her mood..
Little did she know,
That all he wanted was for her to confess her feelings to him..
But nevertheless, just seeing her sad, he let go of his wishes, and apologized for not understanding..
She loved the way he pampered her..
And at times, even if she wasn't sad, she acted to do so, just to see him pamper her ...

Ishika Agarwal

Ishika is a 16 years old girl.
Writing for her is nothing else but a passion. She hails from the city of Joy and Art. She has been a Co-author in 30+ anthologies in the recent past, all adding on experiences to her. Been a part of India book of Record projects like Black and World Record projects like 15 wonders of Poetry, Ishika is paving her way to success.

(1)

Nobody understands my pain. Nobody knows that the spark inside me is vanishing.
Everybody has their dark times, I too have but when is mine going to end.
My life is like a dark neverending road .
I get scared sometimes as I don't have anyone with me .
I need to ignite the spark present within me and then only this dark road ends. I need to think positive then only I will be able to shine bright.
I need to do everything I can to bring that spark back as it can only save me.
I want that spark which will ignite me .

(2)

"Love yourself" people say.
I ask how!
When I can't see anything positive about me or even think anything positive , then how can I love myself!?
Then a person arrived at my front door.
With all the happiness I can contain.
Even in bad situations he would laugh and maintain

Ashima Jain

She is passionate about her work. She is honest. She loves to accept the new challenges. She is loyal. She is most respectful. She is a good listener. She is kind and helpful. She have a good nature. She knows cooking and dancing. She is open minded and openhearted.

Transformation Through Rejection

Rejection... We will face it from time to time... And it hurts. Sometimes rejection painfully rock us to our care, leaving us feeling exposed, lonely and vulnerable.

Rejection means to push something or someone away.

Rejection comes to us in many forms.

Being left out of the group or family,

Being told "" I don't love you "" , experiencing an

Unwanted breaker, not landing the job or positions / not getting into the college, receiving hateful messages on social media being slighted or treated as if you are not there.

One rejection occurs, we typically feel pain in the form of sadness, loneliness, grief and sometimes shame. We all fear the pain of rejection, just as we all fear physical pain.

Rejection can be vicious loop.

Each new rejection reinforces scripts that are based on old hurts, rather than the truth about ourselves, that we are just as lovable and respectable as anyone else."

Gousia Ajaz Khan

She is gousia ajaz, born and brought up in Kashmir, she completed her bachelor's degree in electronics and communication engineering . She strongly believes that the words have the power of healing and changing one's life. She is already working on various anthologies and most of her work is about motivation and inspiration. Penning down her thoughts is her way of spreading positive vibes among her readers.

Instagram id: soulstirring__

Transformation after rejection.

Girl under a night sky wearing a smile full of solace,
Embellishing and Lightening up her aesthetic face,
she wasn't a regular girl who coaxed the worldly race.
She was the one who grew in darkness,
enlightened her soul with her own glaze and brightness .
She ripped off the clouds of loneliness ,
made a home inside her heart full of warmth and tenderness.
She endured all the cruel and harsh seasons of life,
Making her branches blossom like the flowers beautifying a paradise,
Once she used to crave for love and affection ,
gushed out with the tragic waves of deception,
She fell in love with the terrible depths of her salvation,
Ignorant about the shallow rules of love that this world was carved with,
her heart kept on blazing of the actuality and the glaring truth,
loving people silently gave her peace and contentment in lieu of making it loud and abnoxious,
Her reticent and taciturn behavior wasn't acceptable to the frivolous norms of the society,
Trying her best to fit the mould of a typical worldly modesty.
With the growing and flourishing version of her,
she desiderated a person who could see the real person behind her eyes, and effectuate stillness in her world of chaos,
In return only thing that was growing were the piles and pyramids of rejection ,
Sinking beneath the walls of repudiation , she was left cold and miserable.
Left with the scars of replacement, a trough of anguish and the inferno of torment shattered the bounteous heart of her,

for a girl like her it was a challenge for proving herself worthy and laudable,
Bit by bit her feelings were scorched in the flames of desertion and abandonment ,
she deemed it nasty and painful,
Pondering over the voids and splits of her life
she started loathing and questioning her existence,
with despairing and hopeless eyes of her.
To get the answers of all the fiddly questions ,
She instrospected herself to the depths of all her versions,
With the growing and flourishing version of her,
she percieved and appraised the truth ,begging to be loved was self-immolation,
Stuck in the hole of never ending darkness,
a ray of hope dispersed through her soul,
feeling sorry for yourself wasn't a wise thought,
blaming yourself for the tantrums of these dodgy people wasn't a way out,
you're ravishing and beautiful in your own way,
pleasing others wasn't a door to peaceful life,
Making people crave your vibes ,by keeping your potential and attitude much bright,
Prompting and stirring herself with these thoughts ,
there came this night full of stars,
Falling into the daunting depths of her gloomy soul,
burning her scars in the scorching passion of hope ,
She learnt how to keep her head above the nerve racking tides,
feeling things to depths wasn't something to be remorsed or mourned,
She never looked back and never seeked for their attention anymore,
With the deep and fiery holes in her lungs,

She kept on breathing to survive , made everything around her look beautiful and divine,
Turning her infinitely weak spots into dazzling blots,
Putting self love above all, she bloomed like a gleaming flower,
Detaching her happiness from their beliefs and thoughts,
she made a world inside her benevolent
heart ,where self love and inner peace was carved as a piece of art.
"

Kartikeya Chauhan

Kartikeya Chauhan is a 21year old Psychologist and Hypnotherapist. Full of ironies, oxymorons,metaphors, who likes to read people not books. Having seen his share of darkness, he intends to spread light in world with his small efforts.

He writes to heal, give hope and bring change in people. He has been a contributing author in 12+ anthologies , has co-authored two books and has been editor for few anthologies too.

Mountain and Plans.

Sometimes there happens an incident which breaks all our life plans and we make it centre of our future. But is future constructed on our plans? No.

If a climber makes a plan at the bottom of the mountain will that plan be enough to take him to the top of the mountain? No. Infact as he climbs up he faces new challenges, new hurdles, new problems and at each step he plans for next step and at each step he changes his plans cos maybe previous plan give him a fall. He fails to enable the mountain for himself and changes himself for the mountain.

Isn't our life the same? When an individual makes one misfortune incident the centre of his/her life and stop the flow of life, he fails to achieve success, happiness and peace.

So isn't changing ourselves according to flow of life instead of changing flow of life according to us- a way of happy, successful and peaceful life?

Reettika Premjit

A metro -city girl who lives through her dreams. She is a talented singer and a painter. A budding writer, who loves expressing her thoughts through poems, quotes, snippets and short stories. She has served as a co-author in multiple anthologies recently. She aspires to become a great author with her future endeavours.

Instagram handle: @fluttering_tales

LADDER TO SUCCESS

A glimpse of the story of a girl child ,who lived for others in her life .
She was a dark -skin coloured damsel , studying in 3rd grade ,who was a class topper in her previous school .

Her new school was not a welcoming one for her , as she had assumed it to be. She could not make friends and was astray in her own class.

She was an introvert kid and her timid and shy nature made her emotionally sensitive as well . Her simplicity was disliked by many and envied by her mates.

Once she wrote " I have no friends. Really!! ", in her English assignment. The teacher was overwhelmed by this gesture and introduced her to the class.

To acknowledge the request , few students feigned to be polite.
Eventually, she understood that she had to be alone .

She was alienated in her own class . Later, she made a few friends, but they didn't stay for long.
By the end of 10th grade, she went into a state of denial and hated to be around people.
To cope with her stress , she chose the medium of self-help books as she was always misunderstood by all .

She had turned into a social butterfly after she had recovered from her emotional breakdown .

She became a dependable student in her class and took every responsibility with a smile. She was a studious kid , which paved her way to gain success in life.

In her college days , she was the only student from the other state and was ridiculed by her mates for being different.

She took that in a stride but deep down, her agony inflicted the pain .
She suffered from mild depression and her flashbacks , kept her drifting into the pit hole of hell .

Her will power and her plea for help was heard by Lord and she was saved from the clutches of the dark .

She passed with flying colours . Soon after college , she fell in love .
Her love encouraged her to pursue her dreams and slowly she bounced back to life , like a rubber ball.

Showcasing her talents , he had given her the voice to flag her dreams to life.

Over the years of struggle , she had evolved into an affable and compassionate young lady.

Through her strings of hope and perseverance, she never looked behind and moved forward.

She had a few friends who supported her, throughout the journey . She performed yoga and meditation ,to connect with her innerself.

Her story is an inspiration for all those who have lost battles in life.

A broken girl , who pulled off a smile just to make others happy .

And her love for others took her, to serve the silent and unheard souls .

An insight into a life of a girl , who exemplifies a warrior in the battlefield . An aspiring therapist in the upcoming years.

Vidhya Lakshmi

Just a happy-go-girl who loves to pen down the emotions on paper.

Vidhya is a Microbiologist whose life whirls around the kingdom of microbes and their habitat.

Her fad for literature existed in her since she was a child.

She used to write tiny articles and derive immense satisfaction.

Her writing works were published in her school magazine.

She is an active participant in debates at her college's English literature society.

Of late, her love for exploring life-inspiring and mythological books have increased.

Besides, her works were also published in various anthologies.

Recently, she started to write and post in an instagram account.

The page name is @scrawl_down.

The two with skin and blisters.

"The dinner is ready. Help yourself, Akshaya" said her elder sister, Aaradhya. Akshaya, who is younger than Aaradhya by a year and a half has been exhausted after working on tight five to eke out a living, but a call from her solicitous sister restored her energy levels.
"Gosh! It's hard to make the bread and earn the bread at the same time. However, I must be fortunate to have gained a legit position. Way to go, pal. Pull yourself up" Aaradhya summoned herself. The fire in her never seemed to dwindle. She made potatoes- Akshaya's favorite while her thoughts flashed back to that one special evening…
"Stop making potatoes, Aaradhya. Couldn't you be a bit more momentous?" scoffed Akshaya. "But we are broke and jobless and we have nowhere to go" said the perturbed Aaradhya. The two sisters grimaced at their father who got into the scene, wiggling as a consequence of alcohol in his blood. He rested on the worktop that had the picture of his dead wife. The picture was still, yet it vociferated numerous questions for the alcoholic "now I see my daughters struck and withering, the same way you sabotaged my life and bliss" the picture spoke. The intoxicated father ordered his daughters to fire up some exorbitant cuisine to munch upon. "It's just been 2 days after mamma died and all he need is sophistication amidst the depriving financial condition?" pondered Akshaya, yet they are left with zero choices but to serve. "Ewww you're no good in maintaining the royal etiquette, the vegetables are not properly cooked up, useless brats!" chided the father. "I'm gonna grab in some more beverages and pour them down into my liver" he said as he set forth the house.
That was the moment they underwent transformations from rejection. Realization hit them so hard… 'they bite off more

than they chew'. It occurred to them that 'when parents fail to do their job, it is the job of the children to take care of themselves'. They realized that both are equally capable parenting each other. They decided to travel in the road of ups and downs together with sheer tenacity, no matter how worse the road gets.

"This is it, we are leaving. We are born to be extraordinary, not to be subservient. Stuff in your baggage, let's face the world together and prove that we are bold enough to scoop up victory independently. I feel it's not a bad idea to go behind our primal instincts" Aaradhya chewed the cud, bold and brave. The two with skin and blisters buckled up to live life in their own, independent terms… terms that bring the best in them.

The flashback paused when the potatoes were ready. They are the owners of a domicile, a snug car, all in their hard earned money. Aaradhya is going to get married to a suave man, most of the expenses taken care by them. "I'm happy that you're about to face a turning point in your life" said Akshaya. "No, the turning point has been faced already" Aaradhya said, smiling, a smile bright enough to illuminate the room."

Nardhana Ramakrishnan

The writer is a law student who adores the art of wordplay.
She has been writing since pre teens and her articles had been featured ever since in a teen's magazine called Gokulam and got certificates for the same.
She stills pursues writing by writing and posting in the Instagram writing page she owns - Page name - @nardhu_writes
According to her, writing is where she is able to connect with her emotions and feelings the most
She says that the joy of writing is as beautiful as shimmering stardusts
Aside from writing, she enjoys reading books a lot, preferably genres like Fantasy, Romance, Comedy, etc.
She also loves to spend her time in the art of calligraphy

She Coloured Humanity

It was a day where pearly clouds with mild darkness were looming in the sky, blocking the last tinting rays of the sun, with rain drops ready to lash out. Most of them rejoiced, while some saw it with dread & despair, since the weather for them signified like hurt & darkness entwined around their heart, never ready to leave.

18 year old Naira's situation was the same.
Till last year, she loved rains, relished her mom's soup, had chaat with her dad & watch rainbows. But now she weeps due to home sickness.

Naira was 16 when her father lost his job. Since then, things were tough. With great difficulty Naira managed to complete school. She scored well but colleges in Chennai were costly. Their savings were gone too since her father couldn't get a job inspite of attending lots of interviews. So she was forced to study Psychology at Thanjavur, since the fees were low and she could stay in her uncle's house.

But her aunt wasn't too happy with her and made her do chores, and also she had to be home by 6, not roam outside and not bring her friends.
At school she had friends, but here, she had no one.

Now she finished her second year & was happily going to Chennai, eager to be in her mum's arms.
In the late hours of wee evening she saw a gang of rowdy boys eve teasing and troubling a girl. A police officer came and dragged those boys back.
Disturbed by that scene, she got up & comforted that girl. To cheer her up, she took her near the train door and they started to get along well.

All of a sudden, Naira tripped & thought she was about to fall from the running train, when an arm caught her wrist & she turned to look at her saviour.

It was a boy with partial mental disabilities ,working in the pantry car of the train.
Shaking his head & fingers, he said to her, ""Sister, its not safe"" & guided her to the seat to sit & gave her some snacks for free. When she tried to pay, he said, ""You didn't eat anything since noon, eat sister.""

It was a moment of transformation from her rejection
The incident which was her life changing moment leading her to the path of self realization.
Her troubles seemed shamelessly trivial after seeing him.
She reached home. Her father got a high paying job.
She requested her parents to complete her final year by staying at the hostel.
She started her final year, staying in the campus hostel
Her roommates were from different departments & they eventually became soul sisters.
She finished her degree, pursued a masters in Child Care Education in Chennai & became a Special educator, teaching disabled kids.

She realized that in the world where we search for the eroding last drops of humanity, these people though born with disabilities, are blessed with a ocean of heart when it comes to emotions. They aren't just disabled, but specially enabled in their own way."

Natasha Sahoo

NATASHA SAHOO, is 21 years old and belongs to jamshedpur. She is currently pursuing her bachelor of science in nursing and aspires to become an education activist. She has hiwaga Ebullience identity. For her writing is all about motivating and accepting. She is a national level debater. You can read her thoughts on yourquote and Instagram @natashasahoo_06

Scarlet Ignite

You are angry, scared, rejected, lonely, annoyed, exhausted.
You want to be calm, bold, accepted, listened, pleased, supported.
The question hereby emerge,
How will you ultimately merge?
You have gales passed by,
Not all storms come to disrupt but some clear the sky.
Repudiation alarmed you always,
Trying to be normal? Your missing being awesome anyways.
Not that I'm proposing to forget,
Pin every rejection indoor to let your soul ignite to reform your sweat.
Your finding it difficult to stimulate,
Ohh!! Get up and look within to motivate.
It's gonna be easy? It's gonna be fun?
No it's gonna be frustrating and definitely you wanna run.
Rising and diversifying process is painful,
Being stuck where unsuited... What can be more sorrowful?
Be lissome to your life,
Be your own Nutella to survive.
Be the hygge to describe,
Your precious like palos verdes blue butterfly.
Light the intrepid personality,
Prove your potential boundless capacity.
What??? Waiting for someone to appreciate,
Pat your back, head upright, stand strong for the fate you wanna create.

Trust Me

Trust me
I have turned stronger,
Actually more of vehement I add.

Trust me
I have evolved,
""Grow up"" The loud yelling still echoes my dreams,
""Sagacious"" I claim to be thus redeem.

Trust me
Confidence suits me better,
Timid was the role unlikely I played,
Fortunately now it's decayed.

Trust me
I am just not afraid,
Yes horror movies still terrify me,
Definitely not the plethora of judgements I agree.

Trust me
I relish the part of self love,
Actually was blind folded,
Until myself I moulded.

Trust me
I am happy,
Everything around me is colourful,
And definitely there's treasured good for me I am hopeful.

Trust me
I have turned more pensive,

There's no time to be vacant,
Driving into the streets being ambitiously competent.

Trust me
I am oblivious to you,
My priorities have standardized,
Little late... I know!! But ultimately I realised.

Trust me
I am committed,
And it is forever this time.
Now I am the lead and it's my show time.

Vijay Appaji

Vijay is a Mechanical Engineer, who apart from writing also enjoys playing football and watching anime. Writing paved a way to express his introvert self better to the world. Observation of life has always been ink for his pen. He says people who relate to his words and appretiate his work are the sole motivation to keep writing though being a lazy one.

A Knockout To Gear-Up

Like Yin and Yang there is always good and bad about everything and that includes rejections. If you find a good person you may like him/her but as few as their flaws, you would point them out like a black dot on a white paper ignorant of the whole page you can use. Similarly when u find a bad guy, you would be terrified at first but eventually when you get to know him better you would see the little good in him/her like a little star in the whole of dark space.

People who gain success on their first attempt are deemed as smart while people who keep on trying despite the challenges or failure may take time to be called smart but they are more wiser. You might not be lucky enough to start smart but you always have a chance to get back up.

I was pretty bad in studies in my school. I never cared about the marks. I played a lot got punished for not doing homeworks and stuff, been into fights, you name it. So my parents decided to transfer me to another school. Till then i got punished just for not doing homeworks which I didn't care much cuz you know how boring they can be. But for the first time I got punished for getting less marks. I was made to stand outside the class and the teacher hit me with the wooden stick. As funny as it sounds now, that hurt. Well I never felt that bad about the same punishment I got when in din,t do the homework or when I got into a fight with my friend(well he started it! Don't judge me.) but I couldn't digest the fact that the teacher treated me that way because I am not smart enough. I felt so weak and I really hated that. The fighter in me didn't like the knockout i cried when i got home and guess what, by the end of the year I was among top 10 rankers in my whole school. This would have never happened if the teacher didn't reject me. I am very grateful for the day he punished me though I don't like it. If I just dusted off my shirt and swallowed up the humiliation like I always did I wouldn't be the guy I am today.

One can rejoice the success or get knocked out by failure. None need to say how to face success but none talk about how to handle the failure. Well let's not call it failure because it is not. It's just a knockout. Like the one a boxer gives you and the little sparrows and stars flying around your head. Only you get to decide how long the sparrows are gonna fly around you. Knockout does mean you lost the fight. But you would be a failure only if u don't stand up, walk out of the box and start practicing for the next game. Only you possess the power to change the game cuz every knockout offers a chance for you to gear up.

"

Vidisha Agrawal

I am a passionate writer. I love to write what I feel and what other feels too. I write motivational and inspirational quotes, poetry, thoughts and short stories.

Don't Lose Hope

When I face rejections.
Deep down in myself, I destroyed.
I felt struggle in me.
Think, what I have missed.
Am I not well acknowledged.
I faced so many challenges.
Can't share my restlessness.
I broked down inside.
Slowly my dreams have been killed.
What to do and what not.
The question is going around me.
Losing my faith in between.
I try to be hopeful again.
Wish, it couldn't be done.
But have to try again.
I get slowly back into my ambition.
Try another time,
Not to lose hope.
As hope grows strength in me.
What I wanna be is still I want.
Try to regain myself.
I will get what I wanna be.
So I started to find my worth.
Where I have to be grown.
Where I have to be best.
I have started to made best version of mine.
Think, what is the problem in me ?
Hmm, nervousness.
Have to overcome of it.
I have started working.
Sometimes I felt,
I can't do that.
It's quite impossible for me.

But, then asked to me again.
Is there anything impossible ?
No, have to reassemble my trust.
Have started to believe in me.
Started trying to accomplish my dream.
Try to assemble all my broken pieces.
Reassemble all my capabilities.
Recollect all my faith again.
I started work on to the path of success.
The path of my happiness.
Ready to face all challenges.
I took the previous path again.
Again face the challenge.
But this time, no rejection.
Just a lesson of life.
Don't know, what will happen.
I found my path or not.
But one thing I know is.
Not to lose hope.
I am ready to face the result.
Whatever it is, it's just a lesson.
Life is around challenges.
Accomplishments is important.
But, self worth is must.
Don't lose hope.
You will find your way.
You will get what you wanna be.

Leena Saththi

She is an Engineer by profession. Passionate about scribbling her emotions.
Canophilist and a person who lives in the imagination, but accepts reality. She is a Melophile and also loves capturing moments.
She is happy about expressing what others feel.

Justified Rejection

You may be rejected. When it happens to you every single time I know it pricks you so hard.
You might feel unlucky, Wondering why it is always you?
Everyone goes through the phase of rejection at some point in life.

Rejected to get admitted in one of the best institutions?
Rejected by the person whom you love?
Rejected by an interviewer?
Rejected for your looks?
Rejected by a book publisher?
Rejected by the bride's family in matrimony?
Rejected for a job promotion?
The person whom you get inspired by is not that someone who easily climbs the ladder. Just think, You will always be attracted more towards the person who achieved after so many rejections.
So why can't you be the one?
And when you are ready with a mind to face the battle, there are some people out there to mock you down.
It's not a tough thing for them, People are raised up with such a mentality to criticize the person who fails.
They won't look at your struggles.For people your flaws are something to keep them busy.
Just think if life is so smooth,

How can you grow?
How can you improve yourself?
How can you become unique?
How will you get entertained?

Come on sometimes you become the best entertainers for others.It's a good thing right? To entertain someone which is not easy.

People are going to lash you, make you into chunks. Don't wonder why it's always you, because you can brush with death. Every time you're gonna rise and sparkle, making every betrayal as a fuel for your soul.

You will be astonished by the gesture of your loved ones as well.Some may talk behind your back,Some people want to put you down and Some may even join you back when you get lime light.Ignore this negativity.

More than the rejection you are scared about what others might think.Leave this thought right now.You are designed in a unique way and no one can play your role better than yourself.It's your life make it count.

Turn your rejections into a new venture. Definitely you will reach the crown of the hill.

"

Sahina Mamtaz Chowdhury

She's Sahina Mamtaz Chowdhury from Kharupetia Assam, She has completed her Masters and persuing Bachelor of Education.

She has published her writings in 43 Anthologies and going to publish her own book 'Victress' which is a collection of poetry about womanhood.

Tangled

Standing in front of the mirror
I saw an impotent girl and a spread kohl
over her face, and she was trying to
Dislodge it with her trembling hands.
It's me fighting with myself for putting
my mind in a plight and full of sorrows.

I am a strong woman, who stands for herself
But my people pulls me down because I fought
for equality, because I want to fly without any
barriers..

Today, I will not blame my society or my beloved,
It's my fault for letting them play with my life,
Letting them take my decision and for making him
my priority. War, that my mind created is my
doing and today, is the time for taking an action.

She

A thought full of addle jumbled together.
Standing in front of the mirror, the mirror
saw the bewildered look and the smudged kohl
over her face, and she was trying to dislodge it
with her trembling hands.
She screamed and hit the mirror in terror,
as countless voice was raised
to strike her.
She became numb and could see the gore
flowing through her hand.
She was angry, she was weak,
she was impotent but determined.
She thought and thought then
she stood up and made herself
ready to fight against the odds,
because she knew that
this can't be the end of her world
this is just the beginning of new she."

Best Friend

You made my life bright
By shining like the Sun,
We were part of each other
Till I knew you were.

You were my best friend
Shared all our laugh and love,
But what made you to change,
That you wished to betray my heart.

We were together for decades
Prayed for you in all my prayers.
Didn't you thought for once
How your betrayal would break my heart.

Your treachery made me suffer,
Now trust I do not possess,
It would be hard for me to pardon you
Because you were my best friend.

You made me go for the one
Whom you met for an hour,
I was your best not to be left
But you chose your path.

I chose my path too
But after many months of your
fickleness, now when I look back
all I remember is your fake love."

Nishigandha Das

A mathematics teacher by profession. Born and brought up in a small town in Assam. Dreams of being an entrepreneur so that unemployed people gets a way of living. Fond of travelling, photography and also a big foodie.

Never look back

I was 21 yrs old and I just got my graduated from college. I was fat at that time. I am a girl and I was 75kgs. Well too much for a girl to weight. I always regretted of not having a boyfriend in my college days. And this happened just because of my weight. No guy will want a girlfriend who looks like a giant potato. Like other girls, I also wanted a boyfriend who would pamper me, say cheesy lines, do romantic stuffs, but most importantly having some passionate make out and sex. But till now none of those happened. I was 21, single, virgin and hung out with a bunch of guys, and yes, lived in the suburbs with parents. This was my life.

After graduation, I moved to the city for my postgraduation and started living in a student's home. After finally moving out of my parents house, I decided to get a boyfriend. Yes, I sound like a teenage girl. But I was damn obsessed of having a boyfriend and losing my virginity. So, the first thing I did was made an account in a dating app. I had no option. All I wanted was a boyfriend back then.

After a month of texting to the matches in the app, I finally got a date. Yes, a real date, to which I have never ever been to. The guy was named Prithvi, who was a damn fitness freak. After weeks of talking to each other over messages, Prithvi asked me out. He was a kind of short guy with biceps and triceps, and he had a big moustache, like the ancient kings had. It was movie date. After the date, he started to ignore me. I didn't know what actually happened. His messages started decreasing. After a month he texted me about his interest in some other girl and no interest in me. He apologized about this but his sorry didn't work. I was hurt and angry and so I started stalking him in social media. And finally I found the girl Prithvi was interested in. The girl was beautiful, thin, sexy and yes, successful. At that point I realized what happened. I got rejected by a guy because of my weight. And that was my first rejection.

After that, many rejections came and those were because of my weight. This thing was hurting. Guys were rejecting me in the first dates. I was really sad and angry. 6 months passed but I never gave up dating. After almost 20 rejected dates, I met Tarun. He seemed to be nice guy. After a week of talking to him, he asked me out. I was mentally prepared of being getting rejected this time too. But the secnerio was different this time. Tarun was about 5.8 ft tall, dark, had a little bit of beard and he was totally polite and gentle. On the day of our date, I skipped my classes and went to have a lunch date with him. I don't usually skip my classes, but that day I didn't know why, but I skipped my classes. Tarun and I were crazy about street food. So we went to the part of the city where there were only street food stalls. We had our lunch there and later we went to the nearest mall. We walked around there and later sat down on one of the benches there. We talked for hours. We were so much into each other that we didn't know how time passed. We had many things in common. We both were obsessed about hill stations, travelling, street food, photography and many more. When we realized that its late, he came to drop me off to my place. Later that night he texted me, "So, how was today's date? Wanna give a rating?"

I replied "It was pretty good. And the rating will be 4.5"

"4.5? Seriously? I think I was not that bad", he texted

"I know you are not that bad, but bad rating gives a chance of a second date so that you can improve". I replied.

He sent blushing emoticons. Our conversation then extended for hours till late night.

After some weeks, he asked me to be his girlfriend. I became extremely happy and directly said yes to him. After that, talking to him became a habit for me. Tarun made me feel special. I was really happy. Everything seemed to be perfect. We used to go to a lot of dates, walk in the streets holding hands, explored new places of street food, made plans to go travelling together. I loved being with him.

After 4 months we went to the nearest hill station. Well, everything we planned about the trip was well and good except the bookings of our hotel room. I booked two different rooms for us. I did this because same rooms may lead us to have sex and I was not ready. I always wanted to lose virginity but I was not ready about it. Tarun was furious when he came to know about the hotel bookings. He wanted to cancel the trip but I wanted to go. I somehow convinced him to go in to the trip. After a week, the day of our trip arrived. My excitement was its peak. We took a bus from the city to the hill station in the morning. We reached our hotel by night. We checked in the hotel, had our dinner and slept after that in our respective rooms as we were damn tired by our journey. Next day we woke very early, like about 5am, as we had a booking for a trekking to the famous waterfall in the place. The trekking was really adventurous but very tiring. I saw the real nature's beauty during this trekking. Our legs were exhausted but all this hard walking was worth it. Reaching the waterfall all by foot gave me a feeling of satisfaction. Our trekking programme ended by evening. After that we returned to the hotel, freshened up and went to the nearest restaurant. After having our stomach full, we started walking in the streets, holding hands. The feeling of walking in the streets of an unknown place with my boyfriend made me feel special. After the walk we went back to our rooms in the hotel. I changed into my night suit and lay on the bed as I was very tired by the trekking. I took a power nap. I was woken by a knock on my door. It was Tarun. I opened the door and he came in. He then directly lay on my bed giving by me a naughty look. I didn't mind lying on the bed with him. We hugged each other tightly and started making out. Slowly and suddenly he slid his hand under my top. I was shocked by that gesture and directly sat. I was not ready to make love with him at that time. He told me not to worry about anything as he won't be harsh during sex. But I was not ready. We then an argument about it for about half an hour. Unable to convince me, he held my right hand and pushed me to lie on the bed. I was about to shout, but he put his one hand tight on my mouth. He then undressed my shorts of my nightdress and my panty, and started fingering me with the other hand. I then started scratching and beating him so that he let me go. But he tied both my hands by the bed with my shorts and held my mouth so that I couldn't shout. He continued fingering and then slid his penis into my vagina and started banging me. I wanted to shout but couldn't. It was paining like hell. Tears rolled down my eyes in pain. But he did not stop. Tarun continued until he was satisfied. After he stopped, I saw him wearing his pants and leaving my room without saying a word. On the other hand, I was lying on the bed, half naked, tied to the bed, bleeding. I was raped by my own boyfriend. I somehow untied myself later, cleaned myself and sat on a chair regretting about being in relationship with Tarun, regretting about the trip, regretting about everything. Tears were rolling down my eyes continuously. I couldn't sleep that night. At that time what I could only do was to leave the hotel as soon as possible. So, I packed all my things and by dawn checked out of the hotel without having a word with Tarun. I took the earliest bus to the city. After reaching the city, I blocked Tarun in all forms so that he couldn't contact me. I shifted to another student's home so that Tarun couldn't find me. I stopped talking to people. I started to be all by myself. I couldn't concentrate on my studies as I was mentally disturbed by the incident.

I couldn't share with anyone about the incident because we live in India. People here give lectures about justice to rape victims but later blame everything to the girl instead of doing any justice to her, when the girl is known to them. Hypocrite people! It's easy to say to stand up to ourselves, but it's really difficult to when we are victims and we have no support. I was in my final semester of post graduation and I was not able to study. My marks dropped in class tests. I became so devastated that I left my post graduation course and went home. My parents were shocked to see me leaving post grad in my final semester. They started to question me, but I never uttered a word about anything. Months passed by and I mostly stayed in my room reading one book again and again. My parents became tensed about me. They wanted to talk but I never said a word to them.

One day when I was scrolling my social media feed, I saw a photo of a senior of mine captioned about happiness of clearing national level civil services. This post made me do research on the national civil services exams and the posts available. I saw the post of IPS there. At that point I made my mind of clearing it so that I could have an authorized rifle to myself, have bodyguard all around me and nobody could touch me without permission. I told my parents about the civil services exam. They were shocked as well as relieved. They were ready to support me in this. I took online classes of the civil services and started preparing for it. I started working hard for it. After preparing for one and half years, I appeared the exams. The exam had three phases- prelims, mains and personal interview. I somehow cleared the prelims. I worked more hard for my mains examination and I cleared my mains with good rank and got called for personal interview. After a month my date of personal interview arrived. I was very nervous about it. My interview lasted for about an hour. I gave my best in it. After a month the final results came. I was really nervous about it. My father checked the results and he came to me smiling. After giving me a little suspense, he told me that I cleared the exams. My happiness was its peak. I smiled that day after long time. I became an IPS officer. I felt safe after a long time.

I got posted in different state. I never looked back after that day. I never aimed of becoming an IPS, but the incident made me do it. That incident was the turning point of my life.

"

Akhil Kumar Singh

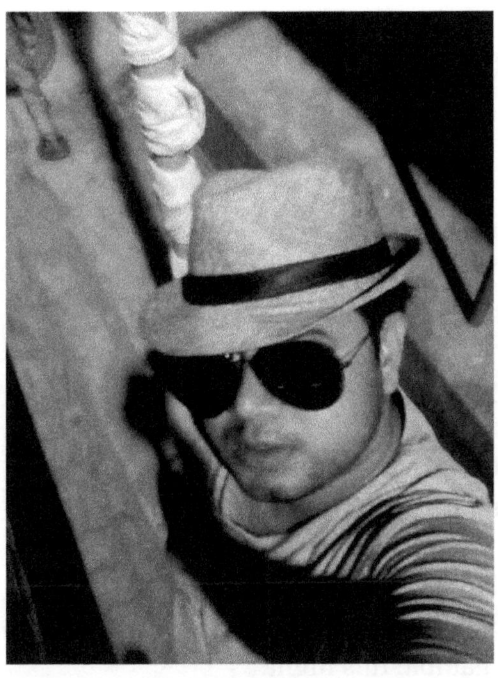

A software engineer by profession, writing is my first love. All those gossips that i hear at markets, at countryside fields, in the bus, that is what inspires me to write.
Just another common man trying to give words to masses and their dreams.

ACT 1

GORY RULES

Betwixt that luring streak of radiance
This global gloom,
Stood in the queue dreams and baggage-
Like educated fools!
Little did i know of this tyrant air
Those badass tycoons,
Bitten by em' now moulded in dust-
So crazy these gory rules!!
P. S.
Honesty my foot gratitude's lost long
Maybe somewhere near toxic woods,
Neither a stain nor an acrid perfume-
Yet all burnt my neat soul its virtues!""ACT 2

SLOW SUICIDE

Lets play a gamble this night,
Teach them all about city delights..
Growing up at forests- kids must survive,
""Never be content,"" flying high beyond skies!
Moneywashed minds intoxified,
One dream not enough next on line..
No time for peace- blink to risk jeopardize,
Exhausting thyself for surplus bread and wine!

""But mumma"" i hate being disguised,
Standing up to expectations everytime..
Crowded streets skyscrapers far and wide,
Been searching for a being trustworthy bonafide!

Out of reach dad's universe- but i tried,
Peers who would leave problems at sight..
Like share markets my stocks fall then rise,
Muted doggie knows it, whimpering whines!
Dressed up neat hair greased with oil,
Plastered smile that childhood exercise..
Sometimes sucks- as if black hole's inside,
Wonder why am jealous of simple folks' life!
Maybe coz they wear their real self all while,
One square meal and yet belching joy..
Stuck up at life's desert- thirsty since nine,
Chasing dreams of all kinds,
Makings of a slow suicide!""ACT 3

NEVER YIELDED

Ever since my tree of dreams
Bore fruits after ages..
Been counting stones from peers
Who masqueraded,
Unaware of wiretapped winds-
Careless mind such naive..
Had lit up those lamps at terrace
Unbounded happiness,
Now when they dig up old cuts-
Copy paste smile on mah face..
Lessons gallore disbanded hunks
Time to breath in brace,
Luminous soul back on streets
Lighting up dark places..
Piecemealing lost grounds buzz be,
""Gosh, he never yielded!

Shri Sambhabi Mishra

Sambhabi is a girl who is hooked up with words ever since she can remember anything. They seem to weave magic that make to be the best kind of miracles known to man. She also enjoys any challenging viewpoints that can keep up awake churning through night. And is kind of looking forward to the remove the boundaries and compulsions that are so integrated in our lives rather wants to live soaring solitary over the vast expanses.

Dawn

It will dawn
For a dawn has to dawn
For all those who wait for the dawn
For who wait for a whisper of dawn
For who wait for their sight to dawn
For who wait for their dreams to dawn
For who wait for a ray to dawn
For who sing the song of dawn
For who mourn that they had lost their dawn
For who murmur the sweetness of dawn
For who never leave a search of dawn
For who will not stop till they get their dawn
For who will not stop till a dawn dawns
For all who wish for a new dawn
For who wish for a dawn
For everyone who has ever missed a dawn
For all those who ask for a dawn
As for every dusk a dawn has to dawn.........

A Secret

The spring does not breathe like that,
It takes you know what,
The patience to hammer a boulder with a needle,
And the will to conquer with that needle.

It takes a blind eye to see
See continuous without a blink
In hope of somehow seeing a sea
And the courage that doesn't think
That it couldn't see the sea...........

It takes the strength to feel
And gauge the heart of steel
And search for a place to steal
In the proud, arrogant steel....

It takes years of wait
And of course never leave the wait
Not giving way to bait
Patiently just work and wait......"

Archa

Archa is gifted with an immensely creative personality. Her major interests are in singing, songwriting, playing guitar and ukulele, writing poetries, abstract art, reading, divination and sky-gazing. She's a queer feminist pagan. Currently, she's pursuing master's in Women's Studies; living a magical life near the Ocean.
Instagram: @goddessiangaygirl
Blog site: moonmermaidmusings.blogspot.com"

What are you afraid of?"" She asked.

Nothing!"" I replied with a smirk followed by a wicked chuckle.

Fear is perhaps engraved into the minds of human beings. The convoluted psyche is weak and fragile. No matter how much we try to keep our fears into the furtive fetters of our minds, it comes out like a flowing river in times of turmoil, treachery or terror. As we burgeon with age, some of us develop the quality of resilience. And, when following the footsteps of our awakening we can realise & release the things we were once scared of.

Who isn't scared of rejection?

The time when our intuition pricks us ""Something bad is going to happen."" It stops us from being vulnerable. But, we tend to listen to our heart discounting our mind.
The heart pounds like galloping wild horses. I can almost hear my beats, like an escalating crescendo. I put all my strength and courage to do things right. But, there's more than meets the eye, that leads me to an exacerbated consequence. I took some hasty steps, and my naivety flips the halcyon anticipation into a nefarious dilemma.

As a consequence, sometimes we face the fulmination of our foolery. We have no choice left apart from coveting desperately to go back in time. We repent speculating ‘maybe, if we knew or were better or the best…’ We tried our best to conquer the quest of our heart's sole desires but due to probable peccadilloes, we bite the dust...

Yes, I was naive. I have taken wrong steps in my past. I can't go back and erase them. I can't quit because resilience won't let me. She's standing right by my side, igniting like a torch in a New Moon night. I take deep breaths, I try to ground myself. I drink water not to quench my thirst but to feel that I'm still alive. I still have hope. Hope to seek further, hope that'll turn my life's chapter. I hear the distant cacophony of my dubious mind, vacillating constantly being flummoxed. But, I push aside the clouds of cynicism - a plethora of pessimistic paucities.

I was born to be daring and confident. The maverick souls don't fade off easily. They try till the end of time. They're sedulous, they're resolute. And, it all became vivid when I grasped the truth - everything is controlled by our thoughts. As we think, as we manifest, things turn out exactly in a similar fashion. Hence, I banished and let go off my past, locking them in my clandestine closet that I deliberately lost the key of.

Fear of rejection doesn't exist anymore. It takes immense willpower, it takes a lot of strength but it's not implausible. Always remember you're the one who can write your own story. So, create it the way you want, the way you desire.

""Nothing?!"" She asked being rather bewilderingly stunned.

""To be veraciously succinct, not anymore…"" I responded while my eyes gleamed with valour and pride.

Harsha Sharma

Harsha Sharma, 23 years old, lives in Jamshedpur. Though a student and a teacher by minor profession, her favourite job is the one she's now doing full time - writing romance. When she isn't writing she is probably dancing and watching Marvel series or probably dreaming of Tom Cruise. As she concludes : Be yourself...

THANKYOU FOR REJECTING ME

Whenever your thoughts arises,
My heart aches.
That countless awakening nights,
And limitless tearing days.
Thankyou for rejecting me
As you gave me the opportunity to shine.

How much should I praise you
For giving me a miserable life?
That haunting dreams
And frightening nightmares
Which shivers my soul.
Thankyou for rejecting me
As you gave me the opportunity to shine.

Now your thoughts will uplift me,
And will take me to zenith.
I learnt to value myself,
Which I had skipped during our days.
The trauma which I am facing today
Will decline after days.
There must be fault in our stars,
Which haunts me everyday.
Thankyou for rejecting me
As you gave me the opportunity to shine.

The darkness inside me,
Still frightens me today.
But there is a light of hope,
Which is increasing day by day.
The pain which you gave me as a gift,

Would always be remembered.
Thankyou for rejecting me
As you gave me the opportunity to shine.

The changes which you see in me today,
Are all given by you.
A new person which you feel in me today,
Is the one gifted by you.
I got new paths to start my life once again,
I lost all that chapters with you,
Which has surely come to an end.
Thankyou for rejecting me
As you gave me the opportunity to shine.

I bid you goodbye for the final time,
As now I lack words to say.
Hope you do well without me,
That all what I can surely pray.
If ever our past haunts you,
Close your eyes and feel our days.
The time which we gave to each other,
And the moment which we spent together.
I wished that you were never mine.
Thankyou for rejecting me
As you gave me the opportunity to shine.

Pragya Rani

Pragya Rani, hailing from Patna, has graduated the 12th grade this year. She is a NEET aspirant. She is a mature teen who loves to ink her imaginations. People believe that poetry is an escape, in her case, it's her life.
She has been a co-author in few anthologies earlier too. She had compile an Anthology for the first time, this year, and looking forward to compile more and more.
She's Jack of all trades, Master of none.

Contact her on Instagram:
@___pragya.___

Happy Reading

THE INTERVIEW

lub-dub, lub-dub, lub-dub' - this is how our hearts' beats when we are absolutely normal but 'boom-boom, boom-boom, boom-boom' - this is how my heart was beating then...
Yes it was the hour of my interview's announcement, we were thirteen candidates out there, and God! The results arrived.
Five people were selected including me and I was so glad. It was my dream company, where I was going to work and learn things. 'the final call letter would be e-mailed and parcelled.' they said and all of us were about to leave when all of a sudden an emergency announcement was made that there has been a change in the list of selected candidates. It said that the three people who were selected, did not included me.
It was the first time, when I got rejected in my life. My heart was broken into billion tiny pieces. For me it was something that not just shattered me from inside, but also created a firework that sooner was going to enlighten the entire industry.
That night, I didn't even blinked an eye, sleeping is way too far. I've never been so alone in my life, all the shits were running in my mind.
Like, ""what if's""and I was questioning my own talent.
Then all of a sudden my phone rang, it was 03:55 and my mom called me, saying she sensed that I was disturbed. I told her everything in that murmuring voice. I needed someone to talk to, I needed her.
I still remember those words she said that day, ""Beti, Rejection is actually good for your personal growth, take it like, you need to improve more, work even harder.
Don't be sad. Go take a nap. You'll feel better. Love you.""
That small talk ignited a fire that day.

Time flew, I got a job in a okay company, duh! I grew and raise it with my mind and heart.

I got promoted, bla, bla, bla... And boom. Now the company who once rejected me, reached to me for help, as my company was the only one to make the highest turnover per year. They offered me, to join their company with the doubling of my salary. I was not a betrayer. I did not left my company. Also, they didn't knew that I'm aware of the secret that it's shares were dropping day by day and none had the potential to save the sunken ship. Alike a business person, I bought 20% of it and then proceeded. Days, months and years passed on, and both of my companies got merged together. Soon I was the new CEO, oh la la! Life was so set.

Having my cold coffee, I wondered how they rejected me in past and now I own the entire company. It's not just under me, but it's with me, so I think about it's progress more than ruling on it like an empire.

""Every rejection leads to some destruction inside us, but remember my dear, this is how you know the worth and enhance your work.""

Abdur Razzaque

Abdur Razzaque has been writing passionately since High School.

He's currently working on his poems collection and about to publish them as soon as it is completed.

He holds a Bachelor of Arts in English from BNMU, Madhepura.

He always says, ""A writer lives in another dimension, you just see a glimpse of him.

Famous personalities and their famous rejections

Rejection is actually a favor in disguise. It's nothing, but a mere word, to someone who believes that there's no losing, only learning.

Walt Disney once said, ""I think it's important to have a good hard failure, when you're young, because it makes you kind of aware of what can happen to you. Because of it I've never had any fear in my whole life when we're near collapse.""

He was fired from a newspaper for not being creative enough, then founded a film studio that went bankrupt before moving to Los Angeles with just $40 in hands but a dream in heart that later created Disney, sooner it turned into an entertainment umpire.

Steve Jobs from Apple itself and later accepted it as a very public failure and due to that rock bottom, he later became CEO of Apple and remained at that post till his last breath.

Oprah Winfrey, famous American television personality, was fired from her first television as an anchor, because not having a face suitable for TV industry.

Steven Spielberg, one who can be easily described as Hollywood's pioneer, with hits like E.T., Jaws, Jurassic Park, Saving Private Ryan, etc. Even he hot rejected from The University of Southern California Film school, not just once, but twice.

Elon Musk, founder of SpaceX and Neauralink, co-founder of Tesla, Solar City and X.com, which later turned into PayPal and having a net worth of around $7000 crore. Impressive, isn't it? A resume, littered with amazing accomplishments with a will of Mount Olympus. But not everyone knows, how many scars he hide behind that smiling face. He had many setbacks, and almost all of them are rock bottom failures.

He launched his first rocket and ""BOOM"", in an instant came the biggest failures of all time with an explosion. But he has a will of Hercules, that's why he's called real life Iron Man. He just don't care about giving up and considered the 2015's explosion as experimental landing issues. See, no failures only learning.

And sooner SpaceX became an open challenge to nasa. Now they are working together on a project, just a few days back SpaceX lifted NASA's astronauts to orbit, a new era of space flight just begun.

But it all started with that one rejection, which made him, what he's today. He said to haven't received any traction when he applied for a job at Netscape company in 1995. They didn't even replied to his emails.

After that he found Zip2 and sooner company's board members turned on him and removed him from CEO. He even once got fired from PayPal's CEO.

These rejections made him even stronger, which later encouraged him to build an aerospace space, to make his dream come true.

Musk once said, ""When something is important enough, you do it even the odds are not in your favour.""

Make rejections leave a positive impact on you, evaluate yourself with it, think on how others look at you, and it can turn out to be empowering. Never regret anything. Regrets are actually What hold us back. Let it all go, it's all about perception. Rejection is a part of life, accept it as a time or moment of learning.

Sneha Kumari

This is Sneha kumari. She has completed his +2 in science. She is found of sports. She loves photography, dancing, reading, painting. She puts his heart and soul into his short stories an love and romance. She wants to lead a simple life. She's into writing since 2018. She has been a co-author in few anthologies before too. Her Instagram handle- _sneha_02510.

Transformation Through Rejection..

A rejection doesn't justify whether I'm a failure or not. Why it happens, that a particular person, whom we do not know much about, reject us and we start to accept us as failures. We think that we cannot do anything further. We hurt ourselves that we did a mistake in knowing someone. While we should not be hurt with rejection. We must make rejection our strength. We should work on achieving success in our life which they can't even think about. They must have to realise that they lost a very precious diamond, a gem, and it can only happen when we stop accepting us as a failure. Don't take rejections as it's some kind of failure, accept it as a part of life, a learning experience.

Believe me, a clear rejection is always better than a fake love, leave it and live.

Riya Ghosh

This is Riya Ghosh from Kolkata . Currently she is pursuing her bachelor's degree from Banaras Hindu University,Varanasi in English language and literature. She has very keen interest in writing . One can know more about her by adding on Instagram _the_wonderer_20

"I was the biggest failure two years back. With a B. Tech degree garnished with wasteful four years of college life, I stood there… waiting for a miracle to happen in my life.. Waiting to change all the damage done.. Waiting for a job.. Waiting for my boyfriend to come back…waiting, just waiting..

I was a mess, literally.

And then, while I decided I would follow my passion, I also realised this waiting won't do.. I HAVE TO GET UP AND RISE AGAIN… and so did I . I toiled hard for one and half years, removed all the negativity from my life and just focussed towards one aim.

And I achieved it. I was one of the firsts to get placed in my college during post graduation.. And believe me, when our Principal announced my name and the whole class clapped…I stood there numb with shock and heartfelt gratitude.. Finally my wait was over..
yes.. It feels exhilarating and soothing at once, when you realise you have risen again. And on top of that, it triggers you to keep moving ahead in life.

As said by someone,completion of one goal is the starting point of another. It is precisely that feeling of never looking back again because you know your worth now. You know what you can do and what you are capable of. The feeling of rising again gives you stability, a ground beneath your feet in life.

Singhetampravalika (S.Pravalika)

Singhetampravalika is from karimnagar she is studying M.B.B.S third year in maheshwara medical clg Hyderabad she completed her schooling in alphores e techno school in karimnagar her passion is to be a doctor and she loves to learn a new things ,good listener , she follows the phenomenon don't think about the fruits of action just do your action as your responsibility and success is not in your hands and she loves simplicity

and her ultimate passion is to serve the nation , empower the woman and she likes to write a poem about struggle of an indian woman

Struggle Of An Indian Woman

Remember,women you were born life giver, miracle creator,magical maker
You were born with the fire of queen and conquerors warriors the blood you bleed
But you were treated badly compare to sibling of opposite gender
You were dodge to give a female birth
You faced many sexual harassments, dowry harassments,acid attacks.the men could not know the pain
You sacrifice your carrier, happiness and live with the responsibility to bring your child and husband to good position
You convert the house to home
You convert the strangers to relatives of your own.
Remember woman , remember your more than you can see
Remember woman, remember your love is endless.
Remember woman , remember you are candle 🕯who burns to give life to others.
Never forget your woman,divine you have been from start

What woman wanted
Long before our grandma was young
Women's fredom was a song not yet sung

Men mostly said that women didn't get it
If you gave them a job they'd just forget it

They said a woman's job was cleaning the house
And staying quiet as a mouse

But many women said we want more

We like our homes,but we want more than chores

We want the right to earn and real pay
We work just as hard as men each day

And more than anything please note
We want to have right to vote

And after the marches and protests were done
All of that is just what they won

Iam a women of a substance

Don't define who iam
By the way I look or the

Clothes I choose to wear

Iam more than what meets the eye
define me by the tough battles
I fight each day

Define me by the courage to face them

No matter how difficult

I value honesty, loyalty,love,respect and trust

I will survive
Despite any struggle

Because iam strong
Through and through

Women

Has fought a thousand battles...
And is still standing .....

Has cried a thousand tears
And is still smiling

Has been broken
Betrayed,abandoned, rejected

But she still walks proud...
Laughs loud....

Lives without fear
Loves without doubt

Woman is beautiful and humble

Every men wish to have a woman as an angel
But you never think you have to create a heaven to the woman

#Respect woman#

Deenu S Adi

Want to become poet,writer and English lecturer. Love to Reading,writing, listening music. Writing is my passion.

Alone With Music

Don't know this world where
sending to me. Because truth is
always be bitter to eat. Hey
people don't hate I say in better
way. Mingle with me I'm also
human being like you. Don't go
with money that's only for few
seconds joy in our life. Be human
first and be kind to everyone.
Your rejection isn't matter but
I love to mingle with all. Beyond that
money there are many relationship.
Those relations are too valuable
in our life. Give value them. Just take
care of those relationships... People were talking behind you
don't take those
seriously just go...go...go...and take
what you want...

Shakti Sinha

Shakti sinha born in Motihari, Bihar daughter of Ashok Kumar shrivastava and Anita shrivastava. She had done B.Tech from Jaipur National University. She have been working in the insurance sector for over 1 years.
She is optimistic and believes in herself, She always keen and eager to learn new things.
Her hobbies are traveling and writting.

(1)

Rejection is always a possibility in our life and how we overcome from this that matters. Feeling rejected is totally opposite of feeling accepted. I had gone through so many rejections in my life at my job no matter other appreciate you or not but you have to believe on yourself. If someone is rejected it doesn't mean that person isn't liked, valued or appreciated for their work. It just means on that time things doesn't work out and there is nothing wrong in that person.

Rejection makes us upset a lot sometimes a little and sometimes more. That time you have to required good guidance and a moral support.

Always try to be positive and this is the way to overcome the negative stuff, because not only does it keep hurting it becomes harder to get past the rejection.

(2)

The rule is simple avoid talking more and more about failures and rejection.

Be in good environment and see everything in positive way.

Negative thoughts never inspire a person to try again .

Stop blaming yourself for the rejection or putting yourself down, you can start believing you will always be rejected.

See the good things inside you try to give some credit to yourself because you took a risk good for you.

You have to understand this everything happen in our life for a reason we not understand right know but things happen for our good only.

Trust the process believe in yourself and do your best .

Do self positive talks and be with someone who motivate you to become a better person and use the rejection as an opportunity.

(3)

Everyone go through rejection in their life but mentally strong people use that pain to grow stronger .
It's depends on person how they take the rejection .
Mentally strong people accept rejections and they accept uncomfortable emotions and deal everything in good way .
You have to accept the discomfort in healthy manner and try your best to achieve goal.
Face every situation with bravery and head on.
Do self positive talks it helps you to overcome the negativity.
Mentally strong people not take rejection as failure they take as compliment.
If you not rejected you may be living in comfort zone, Your thoughts should be positive it helps you to be positive and more focussed in your goals.

(4)

One person opinion or a rejection never define who you are, so don't take it personally takes as a useful compliment and try your best . Your worth doesn't depend on others opinion and you know yourself better than anyone so push yourself and do your best . Be in good surrounding because your surrounding affect and helps you to grow and you get encouragement . Always try to be close with good people your circle defines your growth. Be positive and be strong enough to face any situation don't lose hope just try your best

Cuan Damons

Just an average individual who wants to share his work with the world. He started writing poems because he wants people to learn a lesson from his experiences.

The Art Of Rejection

Rejection brings the thoughts of poet's to life.
We went through pain and the doubts danced in our minds.
We wanted to change reality but it was a hopeless dream.
We realized that with rejection comes a lesson.
The pain will give us strength.
Our experiences will touch other precious souls.
It will be our blessing to the world. "

Lesson One:

I know the feeling of being rejected. You feel disappointed, embarrassed and you describe yourself as a weakling. You feel like your life is a mistake.

Not everything is perfect, you are a flower that is busy growing to blossom in this world. Rejection is a storm you will have to endure. At the end, your growth and perseverance will allow the world to take in your beauty.

Lesson Two:

My friend called me the other day. His first love walked away from him. He was sad and broken. He asked me if I knew how to stop the pain?

I said to him that everything happens for a reason. See it as this, your rejection will lead you to bigger blessings and happiness. Never allow this to change who you are. One day, happiness will come knocking on your

(3)

You held on to me, but not tightly. When you left, I started decaying. Every thought of love disappeared. As I walked to my grave, change took me by the hand and wiped away my tears. I thought I was the problem, but looking at the world we live in, my assumptions were wrong. Now here I am, swimming in wisdom. This sadness is just temporary. There is someone out there, with whom I will share my destiny.

Parul Saxena 'Kehkasha'

Parul Saxena is pursuing Masters in English Literature from University of Lucknow. She started penning down her thoughts under the pen name Kehkasha, about three and a half years ago. So far she had been a part of seven anthologies in both English and Hindi languages; out of those she had compiled three which are titled as— Haze, Aporia and Ye Pal Bhi Guzar Jaayega!?

The Judgementalism

Since it's comfortable for them
What they do is, they judge
They judge us to the point
That we are tricked to believe
That something is wrong with us
As if the one to be blamed is none but us
As if we deserve all the cuss
But is it alright that we think this way?
To get judged or to get swayed?
Just like they are comfortable with judging
Can't we get comfortable and understand this fact
They will judge us no matter whatever be the situation at that
And above all, they will judge according to their wish
They will judge the way they perceived
They won't take into consideration
That even we could've been deceived

All this happens 'cause we are the ones
Who allow them to treat us this way
Who allow them to throw all sorts of tantrums
We are the ones who tell them through our actions
That we get scared by their judgement
That we care, more about what they say is right for us
Than what we think is
We are the ones who give them these chances
Who shout loudly in front of them by getting depressed
By falling into their traps and getting supressed

You call 'them', 'the Society?'
I call 'them', your 'Fears!'
The ones that were hiding deep inside your heart

Like a coward
Waiting for 'someone' to give them a voice
This 'someone' might be the society
But their words are your heart's choice
The deeply burried nonchalant noise.

Sufficient Rejections

Failed about fifteen hundred times
Tried over and over again
He gifted us the light bulb
Addison was the name
He had the courage to get rained on
With the tantrums and mockings
But most of us are rather coward
Not like some weaklimgs
But someone who had lost his powers
To face, to get up and not be enraged
To learn from rejections
And to come out of the mental cage
What we do is we try to change
Not just the faliures but ourselves
'Cause we don't want more objections
'Cause we've had sufficient rejections
But is this something supposedly to be done?
Is it okay to let them alone have all the fun?
Fine! Rejections are the part of life
But not the only reason we survive
So in stead of letting it change the game
Why not we use it to build our fame?
In stead of changing and loosing ourselves
Why don't we let the situations change
Not to get afraid, not to feel the rage
Just deal with perfection, if rejection is the cage
Tell the world that we have no extra page
To bother or write, about the despicable tricks
We've had sufficient rejections
Which in our hearts really prick.

-

Punit Dubey

Hey peeps! This is Punit Dubey from Varanasi. She is the one who believes in love and independence. And love to write down her soul to set herself free.

And her writing is to set each and everyone free from their emotional baggage.

Thank you.

Introduction

This is a story of the young girl who fought like a rebellion to the society for her love. But after years, the love of her life left her too. So, this is as a whole description of her roller coaster of her emotions that she went through over years. And still managed to become and independent with a pen and paper in her hand to accept everything and fly like a bird, with her wings open up to the sky. To chase the happiness even while suffering through the darkness.

I request you all to read it whenever u feel alone or lost. My words and my examples are always there for you to stick to your life. It's a story about accepting the facts and changes the world is giving to you and no matter what happens. Accept your faith and journey of life.

The Teenage Shit

I have always been a dreamer, you know? But in a world draped in illusions. I have always tried not to let it show.
I think it is the only place, where I can be myself anymore. Where I can wrap myself in all my fears and firmly lock the door. But I do realize that there are these little windows, some, that inadvertently betray me. Some sadistic smiles that grow writer in me and as my memories forced me to into this submission and flag me.
I try not let it break me, but I can't hold on for long. The world needs to realize that it is wrong. And I am strong enough to drag my feet along the lines of shear agony.
As I write this note, I realize I am not only the one who sits in corner on rusty iron bench and cried because people around me looked at me with contorted faces. It is hard not to break, it is harder not to let it take a little part of me away. But inevitably it does.
I remember how everyone looked at me, when I came back home after running and fighting for my love. One by one, I tried everyone's luck as I punctured their bubbles until they burst. Some took it for aggression, some mistook it for bitter pride, others said if they looked in my underpants, they would find a ""D"" inside...I didn't mind. I thought with time, it would subside. But the voices outside and inside my head have since, never died.
I remember, 16 years old eye, being overpowered! The power that was gained by the tears and hatred, not only from the society but also from those whom I called my friends. Yes! I did a mistake. I ran away from my family to chase the ray, that was not meant to be my Bae.

For the one I found as my love, life, sun, moon, family, friend, smile, fear, cry, betray. Every time we fought, I found him around. Everyone who liked me a lot doesn't liked him anyway, as he was an orphan. According to society, orphans aren't allowed to love. But it is wrong, the society was wrong. So being a rebellion, I ran alone, that day. Alone for all the love that we both carried and all the hatred and aggression my people carried for us.
But unfortunately, my parents caught me with the help of police and him, as I was too young to be a rebellion. But then he left, but not forever. He came back, back after 21 long days. Then we stayed as lovers, as family and as friends for years.

But the life is meant to change. Change is the salt of life and power of acceptance is the sugar. Balancing between the High BP and sugar, now what we called life. So, he left! left me after sharing all the love and care because of that myth of being an orphan and losing the love. Now he is a half-written story in my book and I do not want to tear. Since then, it took years for me to re-build my confidence to love and self-defense. I have locked myself inside and wallowed in self pithy. I behaved like abnormal, until I find that normal in me. None will feel the goose bumps on my skin, whenever anyone mention about the love, sweety. It's okay to fall in love to such tender age, it's okay to fall out of love at time you are getting married. Everything is fine until you faiths are divine.

So, if you ever feel of falling down, just look at me. As I am an 25 year old independent woman who has the courage of writing her own mistakes loud. Now, I have a courage to live with people around with their so called "love-marriages" who once hated for the same. May be me and my love aren't meant to be together but he built inside me is unbreakable. No matter what, love "LOVE", no matter what respect that "LOVE". As I write this, I maintain that I still like to dream. It is what I am. It is what I always have been. Call me ignorant, call me anything sharp or blunt. But if you can't understand the devastation and it's theme. I suggest you to leave, leave me to myself and to my dreams. I have illusions to make, delusions to chase. I have memories to confront, and I have nightmares to chase.

The Meaningful Nothingness

I desire to write and spell,
Being an observant, it feels like,
All the words are unmeaning and so are the sentences...
Where to start, where to end.
These amorphous notions are not letting me impel.
So, what do you think I need, A pen, a paper navigator???

Oh, my dear the answer is around everywhere...
Neither a pen nor a paper, all we need is the will of go-getter.
Removing illusions of all the motion,
Its time you get your things back to motion...
Being an observing, you write and spell,
finding meaning in this nothingness, it's time you go and get your gear.

Kancharla Sai Sandeep

This opportunity has provided to share his feelings

Life Of Ram

We may notice the pain of a mother
For her 9 months to introduce a child
But we may not notice the pain of a father
Who thinks about the welfare of his family, concerned.

Born in a middle class family
Bought up by her mother bravely
His father never took enough care
And life had become a nightmare

His life has been balanced with pleasures and trails.
He had many tear drops and thousand of smiles
Life is relentless struggle
As it was full of troubles
Pain and egony is at each step
Yet he tried to rise without fear of blow or slap

Everyday from his first sight
He thinks of his brothers and for their careers to be bright.
Thought the situations are tight
The future he went came light from the dark bright.

He stands having fulfilled his brothers dreams today
But he had suffered plenty chasing them everyday.

Though he faced many challenges
he had deal those with his courageous
For many years he tried so hard
To live a life.... a normal life
But he can't escape from the dark shadow
Which is creeping behind him

For many years he tried to hide
Fighting with his battles quite inside
Afraid to say something and open up
About his shadow that's taking over his life
Fearful of being judged and misunderstood
He thought hiding it is for the best
Though the Shadow didn't gave him rest

He had grown like a cocoon
From a baron to a tycoon
Life is full of twists and turns
It's of ups and downs
The struggle you feel today
Will offer the strength you need tomorrow
Start upward and then move ahead
You will go where you want to in life
Don't think about the past
Think how to handle the rest
If you look down you will have to repent
Choose your own path and find your way
You will also have your say
Move ahead and things will be fine
That is why it's called life."

Priyadharshini (Abi)

Priyadharshini Anandan her pen name is Abi. She is an Engineer working an Aerospace industry and she is budding writer, co-author for English and Tamil anthology books. As a writer she believes that words written have more power in bringing up any change.

Trans Angel.

Her voice is not as sweet as a nightingale,
Her skin is not as soft as flower petals,
Her appearance holds great aesthetics,
Her eyes are always filled with high resolute,
Her desires were always obtaining her reverence,
Her destiny was always her identity,
She never gave up on being herself,

She was always building her when people were demolishing her with repulsiveness and vilipend,
Even when she was shamed by people she shaped herself with her confidence,
She harmed people who harmed her feelings and also she mystically enchanted people, who trashed her feelings too.

She was her own queen always, no matter what others words for her,
She never bowed her head hearing mortifications done for her,
She always stood stoned afore the stones thrown at her, so that she never slips her crown down.

She struggled to be in her own world in this judgemental world,
She who never gave up on her dream to be a girl, differently from others,
She is resplendent by her strong vigor,
She just inspires us to be our own self no matter what.

When everyone in this world running to heedfully aurally perceive others applause to them,

She does it for herself by her claps, she inspires us to be self-motivated,
She is so strong and magnificent maybe because,
She is a ""She"" from ""He"",

She is also a she who needs to be empowered and treated equally.

We should owe an astronomically immense reverence as she deserves it,
In earth all are living beings,
All become human beings by integrating humanity,
Humanity isn't accommodating or availing, it commences revering each one's emotions.

We are in this together, we shall not break her wings,
She has other options to come back with her broom,
She and her emotions are to be venerated,
Our gestures may bring up the changes what they require.
The potency of the third gender is equipotent to the potency of third eye.

Deborah Esther

Deborah lives in Coimbatore pursuing her degree in B.A English literature.

She is fascinated to write and sing. She loves simplicity. Her dream is to inspire People

Time To Change

Black or White ,we all are same
Rich or poor , love measures us.
Good and bad doesn't matter,
How you treat yourself matters everything.
Be deaf to gossips and appreciation,
Focus on what's your destination.
Your destiny is in your choice,
Make it wise to shout your victory in loud noise.
Rejection and failures are like oxygen,
Which makes you breath to live your life.
Mistake is not a big mistake,
Repeating it is a great fault.
Pursue positivity, evade negativity
Always show gratitude,
That makes you reach multitudes.
Deborah."

Ayushi

Hey Lovely Readers, I Hope You All Are Fine In This Pandemic Situation In Your Home. I know you all are feel boring in your home so she's here with her some work. She Is Ayushi. She Is From Prayagraj,Uttar Pradesh. She is still a student. She's here to present her work. I hope you all will like it. Thank you

Time

Time Is The Most Important Thing In This World...
If You Use It As Your Powerful Weapon you can become a better person than others
You will achieve anything in your life which you want
They say good things take time so be patient with what you want
We should not have time to hate people who hate us because
We should be too busy loving people who love us
Sometimes it's better to be alone.
Nobody can hurt you!
don't waste your tears on people
Who don't know the value of your tears
Good times and crazy friends make the best memories so be busy with them
Time never stop for anyone
so just go with it if you don't go with it,
It will never wait for you and you will regret it later...

Ayush Manot

This is Ayush Manot and he's a lazy dumb introverted boy. He is convinced that no poem can do justice to the taste of Jalebi. He doesn't speak much neither shares his emotions much so he converts them into words. He love being pampered but still he knows how to cook, sing, dance and write. He's an emotional child who just passed first year of degree.

Don't Stop Loving

Maybe she wasn't the one,
Maybe she wasn't just made for you,
Maybe she couldn't give you the happiness you desire,
Maybe you were just attracted to her,
Maybe you were just ignoring her dominating behaviour,
Maybe she wasn't meant for you,
But,
Surely there is one waiting for a guy like you,
A guy she craves for emotional attention,
A guy with beautiful soul and heart,
A guy whose behaviour overpowers his appearance,
A guy she wants only for her,
A guy who would take care of her,
A guy who is a little shy but also flirty,
A guy who is intellect Yet isn't dominating,
A guy who is not perfect but perfect for her,
A guy who would take care of her during her periods,
A guy who would hug her and say ""it's going to be alright, I'm here"" when everything is falling apart,
A guy who would team up with her against any difficulties even if it is the problems or fights between them,
A guy who would wake her up in morning for a long drive and end the day watching the sunset with her,
A guy who is a kid and needs as much attention as he gives to others,
A guy who would prefer ""Netflix and chill"" over going to clubs and parties,
Maybe The girl you loved the most was not right for you,
But you got a really good girl waiting for you,
So don't you give up hopes on love,
Love is sacred,
Love is holy,
Love is what makes the world lovely.

Deepanshi Sarwal

Currently a Student of Bsc medical
Owns her own writing page__gibzia_pens__
A wandering soul who always want a chance to explore more and gain experiences.
Loves to travel.

A True Warrior

Listening to my heart
I followed my dreams
Believing in myself that
I am not less than any team.

Rejections come in everyone's part,
Nobody bothers how passionate you are,
Struggling will lead me to success one day
All I could focus is not to miss any dart.

Times of blooming occured finally
All my hardwork payed off,
New journey started,now no plans to stop
Climbing success leader I'll be on top.

There's no need for me to proove myself
I have potential to shine bright like a star.
Haters gonna hate me everyday
But now I am not afraid of getting scars.

Tiered of being stabbed and betrayed
Experienced so much, now none I need
Completely ready to face any battle
I am a fighter not a damsel in sheild.

A Story Of Love And Pain

Trusting someone is very easy
But their betrayal is quite vicious.
Forgetting about them is little hard
But their deeds make you ambitious.

Non-acceptance of your close ones
Feels like needles pierced into heart,
Not ignoring the other side of cause
Must be good that you drifted apart.

Being a slave to someone and
Tolerating their infidelity
Rather
Be a renowned brand which
Maintains your own dignity.

It's necessary to be in such situations
Helps to get yourself polished,
You learn to read faces and deeds
Because experiences are their to admonish. ~

Don't Loose Your Heart

Rejections are a phase in life
everyone has to go through them,
No matter what efforts you've put
everyone has to try a bit harder.

World is so cruel, it will
always let you down,
Surrendering yourself to it
is not a solution we count.

Be a warrior and fight back, Peep into yourself and trust your ability.
You are not a Rebel without cause but a person who maintains their stability.

Don't loose Your heart God has plans for you
wear a bright smile accepting your shortcomings.
Try and try with great enthusiasm and passion
opportunities will be awaiting.

The Anxiety Problems

Ideal mind is a devil's workshop
Occupies our mind with overthinking,
Thinking of scenarios, would never happen.
At last in sea of depression we're sinking.

Slowly slowly drowning completely,
No idea how to handle mood swings,
Random thoughts give heebie-jeebies
Friends are the one to whom we ping.

Get up lazy Jack and try to
Overcome unnecessary thoughts
Sing, Dance or Cheer up with mates
And fill up all your anxiety droughts.

Learn to thank God
For every breath you get,
Don't ruin yourself panicking
Because whole life is to live yet.

Bheemparam Kishore Kumar

Even though by profession is a Medico at Kakatiya Medical College, Warangal. he is one among the passionate writer comming up with his talent fresh words. The way he frame his lines perfectly go in sync with the content. He has worked as Co-author for 5 anthologies.
He is always thankful to his friends & family as they in each step supported in writing in improving himself.

""He believes the art of saving lives inspires in making art of everything he can. When you feel the things happening around you, every word you speak can be made an art of it.

I was 18 aiming to crack Medical entrance..
tried for an year but failed at first attempt..
waited an year again & gave my better try..
& yeah failed again..
People atarted to lose hope & trust in my capability..
But never bothered & prepared mentally for another try..
convincing parents with hell of conditions..
On attempting entrance, results were out on 14th day..
Yeah! successfully got rejected again with a border of 2 marks..
felt ashamed, depressed, no words left to explain..

Joined agriculture as promised on condition if failed again..
Native changed, New friends, New fun..
but the guilt of being lost never faded away. With a new ray of Hope changed mindset & started preparing for exam in silence. Exam day arrived in about 5 months.. Stress & fear started ruin my confidence levels.. leaving everything behind.. Meditated for a while & gave my best shot.
Results were out in no time..
& Yeah!! this is the most emotionally stressed out moment filled with excitement & tears.
But this time everything has changed.. Parents whose eyes were usually filled with pain & sadnesa were now filled with happiness & excitement.
Friends & Family who criticized & mocked at my failure now strated to praise & congratulate for setting an examole for hardwork & believing in dreams.

Rejections might change every aspect of life..
It could even bring you to a phase
where you no more feel like living..
But things that only things that live up are
Hope & Trust which brings you Up.

Life rejected him..

Pushing him to the edge of every path he choose..
reached a point where
rejecting Life was the only option he had..

Planned & Executed for hanging down to death..
A moment later on opening eyes
realized even Death's rejecting him...
Then point of gyan stricked him
being alive and rejected by death must have
a underlying reason..
Then started to pendown his emotions & experiences
of being rejected giving his life a massive break through..
There is a wild cry in every word he expressed

(3)

Never ever in Life
You can learn from success stories..
Yes I mean it.
The more we focus on Success stories..
the more you feel things easy..
50% passive chance of overconfidence
misleading a wrong path.

But focusing a failure or a Rejected stories
making you aware of hurdles from Ups & downs..
Leading 85% probability of being Successful."

Soumith Reddy Pingili

Dr.P.Soumith Reddy is one of the upcomming Doctor by profession. He also proved himself with his skills of wordings. Soumith believes he can create another dimension with his words.

Pains of mine are known to the inks of a pen which made a flow for these lines
In the shades of darkness..Shadow of a person..
Remembering and recollecting the tiny things he underwent..
He tried shortcuts and even shortcuts for shortcut..
He is neither afraid of anything nor sucessful of everything.
All he wished is to live a wealthy life ruining his healthy life..
Addicted to rejections only rehabilitation was sucess..
Many questions but his only answer was rejection..
His Struggles as pebbles of an ocean..
Worst things made him a better person.. As the shades of darkness shaded away..
He's known for his failure's..
Everyone around says how to live.. but doesn't live his life
As a ray of hope.. Every thing he transformed was an offer of rejection..
But not everyone can transform from their rejections..
But everyone can reject their rejections..
His only word was ""rejections are not failure's but they are just Objections ""
Stable mind and determination what matters
When you target a high flying bird.

(2)

Sky has limits but his happiness doesn't know limit..
He's good at everything ..in his world..
His parents as his world..
Ranking high was his routine work..
Flying high is just a small thing for him..
He's known for his success..
Mistakes of him considered as miracles..
His normal works are amazing works for everyone..
Rejection was not a word even in his dream..
Rejection of others is a matter of nothing for him
Days passed as clouds fade away..
In thundering silence a word stepped into his world..
His little mistakes are worse things ever..
Everyone criticize for his good deeds too ..
Rejection as the word day and night..
Tear's as his dear friends unknown to everyone..
His dream profession as far as sky..
Pain in rejection as Pain in his veins..
Heart with full of broken pieces..
Confused about which piece to be followed..
Still stubborn in winning his dream profession..
Making his blood as sweat..
Knowing down people words..
Making his parents proud..
Then.. Answering a question..
""Why can't you find a successful path? ""
""Finding a path for life doesn't mean follwing sucessful path of others but to make your path successful ""
Path may be filled with struggles.. Rejections..which sets your life as an example.. ""A normal person can be a great by climbing a single step up than others

(3)

Obsessed with success Impermissible for rejections..
Addicted to success stories ..
Unwilling to learn from failure stories..
Habituated for success stories
Independent on self stories..
Not scared of dark but scared of what's in it..
Not afraid of heights but afraid of falling..
Not afraid of love ,just afraid of not being loved back..
Not afraid of people around.. Just afraid of rejection..
Not afraid to try again just afraid of getting hurt for the same reason..
Realising rejection as not a failure..
Stepping to reach high..
Transforming to live high..
From nothing to everything..
Criticism from people to compliments..
Rejection is a part of everything but rejecting and learning from the rejection that makes you anything..
Great minds doesn't evolve without rejection.. But learning from it makes them..
A single step different from successful and normal person is transformation through rejections what makes them.."

Mahammad Rizwan Ahamed

Rizwan is passionate part time writer. He writes to express rather than to impress and looking forward to express himself more.

Mail Id: rizwan.29092@gmail.com

Be Positive Even If You Are Positive...

April 18th 2015
I was in chilled climate with spine chilling corpses around me. My own feet were pulling me down. My numb soma was refusing to make a move after reaching 2196ft above the South Col calling up my fate before 769 days.

My name's Adweta Iyer. I was a simple small town girl with lot of aspirations and zeal to achieve something big in life. I was very precise about what I was doing. My parents braced me all the time. My father was a GDS at Siruvalur in Ariyalur district, Tamilnadu. My mother was Homemaker. Whenever I had a complication they were there reassuring my solidity. I have a younger brother who fought with me a lot but cared me a lot more than that. I was a bright student at school and was appraised by teachers for my works. I was a sporty person and a sportive person. I used to participate in all the games irrespective of winning or losing. I did not see myself as a winner or loser in the game but as a player in the game. This was one of my attribute that contributed for my friendship. I had many friends who were cheerful, warm, welcoming and sometimes annoying as well. I was having a lively and contended life. I was on my own path for my career.

March 10th 2013
This was the day when something miserable happened which brought an upheaval into my balmy life. It was like an unexpected vulnerable catastrophe on a spring morning. It was like gloomy dark clouds seizing the moon's light on Full moon day. It was all because an uninvited host entered my life that I was not aware of. I was tested HIV positive. This news spread in the village more rapidly than a pandemic. Every

idiot was assassinating my character. My mother was called a brothel keeper. My father received a lot of blame. He was said that “A man delivering covers couldn’t provide a cover for her daughter”. This was the time when all my friends whom I bothered a lot were not with me. They were all moving away or being moved away from me. It was no wonder as even my own brother whom I cared a lot was forsaking me. I loved going to school but my teachers whom I thought to be wise and intellects and whom I adored also isolated and treated me as an untouchable. I tried to explain my own family that it was not my fault and I did not commit any sin. I attempted to tell them that I am pure but all my efforts were a vain. They did not believe me. That broke my heart and collapsed my mind. It was no surprise that the outsiders detested me. My relatives also knew about this and I was lost. I was no one to live here and had nowhere to go. My family was fed up with all the allegations from all around. They were hinting me to leave home but they couldn’t tell directly as they were parents. I was implied and compelled to leave the house.

May 3rd 2013
Finally I left my house and reached Mumbai with a bag on my back and burden in my mind. I reached a new town. I never stepped out of my house alone like this. Here it was really tough to figure out livelihood in a busy town because I was a minor and tougher because I was a girl. My survival became much tougher when some foxy brats tried to take advantage of my gender and my situation. However I escaped from those troubles with great difficulty. The temple steps and the pavements became my residence.

May 26th 2013

It was 23rd day of this new life. All my money I brought was over. I was exhausted and all my dreams shattered at once like a cardcastle. It seemed impossible to exist. I never thought an unsterile needle from an irresponsible doctor would affect my life to this extent that it would force me to extinct. So I went on to a cliff top nearby and decided to kill myself.
Before committing that heinous and foolish act I introspected myself. Then my soul prompted me if you have the courage to die, use it to live my dear. Do not bother about the shattered cardcastle, build your rock solid concrete skyscraper this time. You were a player who did not care about winning or losing. So don't complicate. Just get into the field of life and play. There are a lot of chances to die but only one chance to live. Everything seems impossible UNTILL IT'S DONE. Then I realized and accepted my fate made a decision to move on.
It was easy to convince my mind but more difficult to convince my stomach. As thoughts do not feed stomach food does. My stomach was growling "HOW LONG?" . I had no answer. But I managed to answer it with the left overs at scrap. Then I made my living through different works at various artisans. I worked as a janitor for living. I was surviving but I wasn't living. I wanted to achieve something.

Sept 29th 2013
That was the time I decided to start a chapter of my life. I aimed to climb the Everest. Yes, the Mount Everest. Then main adversities started. I worked harder to collect money which caused me more ill-health. Then I knew I was having a regular treatment for my ailments and human immunodeficiency virus. My ill-health was recovered but virus was very loyal, it stood with me. Later on, I went for the registration as mountaineer.

Feb 27th 2014

My training went well. I got permission to climb my dream Everest. But a nightmare occurred in the form of earthquake and crashed all our hard work. So for that year the expedition was cancelled. Again I was back to my despaired life and again the life as same untouchable worker.

March 8th 2015

It was the time we got back to our camps and got ourselves better and started our expedition. After crossing Basecamp, Icefall, Lhotse wall, South col I was exhausted with a few more meters left to summit. My body said you can't but my brain cussed you should. My soul prompted you didn't do all this to give up.

Then I pushed myself, reached the top, stood on the apex of Mount Everest facing the bright sun and shouted loudly "I did it". The sun rays replied ""You are like your name Adweta - inspirational and idealisitc"". Those were the rays of hope. This untouchable girl held and waved the Indian flag. I wished that I should return safely to share my story with you all and try to spend my rest of life with my family. I returned and am sharing my story.

I just wanted to say "The climb may be tough but the view from top is always better".

Be positive even if you are tested positive. Never ever lose hope

Flairs & Glairs

Flairs and Glairs, a platform by a student for the students. We are esteemed youth struggling to carve out our path for our future and we follow a basic mindset Since everyone is not born with all-round skills. Joining hands with people who are born to execute it with perfection is the best way to evolve. Self-Evolution is the need of the hour but, evolving as a community is what we strive for. The initiative as kickstarted by, Founder- Mr. Shubham Shah with the motive to utilize the skillset and talent of writing has now a team of 10+ people who are actively participating into newer forms of learning and discovering talents among youngsters. We Provide platform and services like Publishing opportunities, Open mics, Workshops, Hands-on training. Operating with Brand Name Of Flairs and Glairs (Publication House), we offer the chance of elevating a passionate writer to an esteemed author With Brand name Teekhe Zasbaaat, We bring to you an opportunity to get accustomed with the Public Speaking and Presenting of Thoughts along with regular challenges to brush up your inking spirit. The newest initiative to extend our services we introduced in a new writing Platform- The Glittering Fables and Ink Over Tears.

We Choose to Fly Like A Falcon than to be a

Leg Pulling Crab.

To Know More: Infoline – 7781900870
Mail Us At-
flairsandglairs@gmail.com / info@flairsandglairs.in
Or Visit is at
www.flairsandglairs.com / www.flairsandglairs.in
Social Handles- @flairsandglairs @teekhezasbaaat

www.ingramcontent.com/pod-product-compliance
Ingram Content Group UK Ltd.
Pitfield, Milton Keynes, MK11 3LW, UK
UKHW022004190726
13853UKWH00004B/1733